This book belongs to

_____

Published by Scholastic Inc., 90 Old Sherman Turnpike, Danbury, Connecticut 06816.

ISBN: 0-439-87924-8

Printed in the U.S.A.

First Scholastic printing, September 2006

THE CHICKEN NOODLE SOUPER BOWL

A Lesson in
Being Patient

by **Doug Peterson**
Illustrated by **Michael Moore**

SCHOLASTIC INC.

New York Toronto London Auckland Sydney
Mexico City New Delhi Hong Kong Buenos Aires

It all started one cold, cold morning. A Viking ship sailed up to everyone's favorite fast-food place—Barbarian Burger.

"Welcome to Barbarian Burger. May I take your order?" said the voice over the sail-through speaker.

"Uh . . . we'll take 15 Barbarian Burgers," said Olaf.

So far, so good. In fact, everything was just fine *until . . .*

Everyone in the boat started yelling
at the same time.

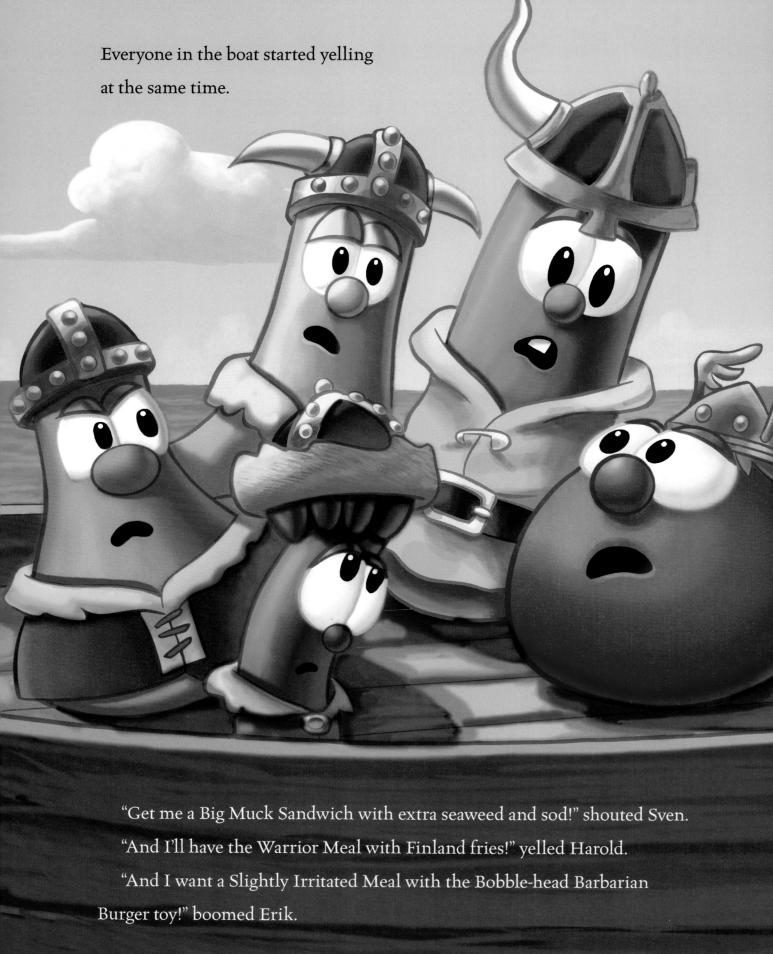

"Get me a Big Muck Sandwich with extra seaweed and sod!" shouted Sven.

"And I'll have the Warrior Meal with Finland fries!" yelled Harold.

"And I want a Slightly Irritated Meal with the Bobble-head Barbarian
Burger toy!" boomed Erik.

"One at a time!" Olaf shouted.

But "one at a time" quickly became "five at a time." No one would wait his turn, and everyone started pushing and arguing. Things couldn't get any worse *until* . . .

9

Suddenly, another ship rammed right into the side of the Viking boat, almost knocking everyone flat on their faces. The other ship was being steered by the famous Cheese-Packers, a group of wild gourds from Wisconsin. They were delivering "gourda" cheese to Finland. As everyone struggled to their feet, the Head Cheese asked, "Mind if we cut in line?"

CRASH!

"We were here first!" declared Olaf.

"Too bad!" the Cheese-Packers shouted.

The Cheese-Packers swarmed onto the Viking ship. Then they all started pushing

and shoving, trying to order their food first. Just when things couldn't get any worse . . .

. . . a huge Wisconsin gourd leaped onto the Viking boat

and smashed right through the bottom of the ship.

"Oops," said the gourd.

Loaded with Vikings and Cheese-Packers, the ship began to sink.

"Quick! Everyone onto the Cheese-Packer ship!" Olaf shouted to his men.

So everyone leaped onto the Cheese-Packer ship—including the huge gourd.

"Oops," said the gourd.
As the Cheese-Packer ship
also began to sink, the Vikings
and Cheese-Packers swam to shore.

Then all of them tried to squeeze through the front door of Barbarian Burger at the exact same time. The Vikings and Cheese-Packers smashed open the door and stormed the counter.

The teenager at the register just stared in pure terror.

Lyle the Kindly, the smallest Viking of all, hopped onto the counter and spoke up. "Hold it! Hold it!" he cried. The Vikings and Cheese-Packers came to a screeching halt.

"We've got to be patient!" Lyle said. "Being patient means waiting your turn, and it's better than fighting. God tells us that being patient brings peace."

"But does it bring food?" shouted Bjorn.

"We want food! We want food!" the warriors chanted.

Lyle whispered to the guy behind the counter. "How long will it take to get the burgers ready?"

"That's the problem," the worker whispered back. "George the Hamburger Flipper just went home sick."

"We want food! We want food!"

George the Flipper was sick? This was the worst news Lyle could have heard. If he couldn't get these warriors to wait for their meal, they were going to tear the place apart.

"Be patient," Lyle pleaded. Then he whispered again to the worker. "Is there *anything* else you can throw together?"

"Uh . . ." the skinny teenager muttered. "I . . . uh . . . can make a pretty good bowl of chicken noodle soup."

"That's it!" exclaimed Lyle. Then he turned back to the Cheese-Packers and Vikings. "George the Hamburger Flipper is home sick. But wait! We're going to get the finest chicken noodle soup in the land."

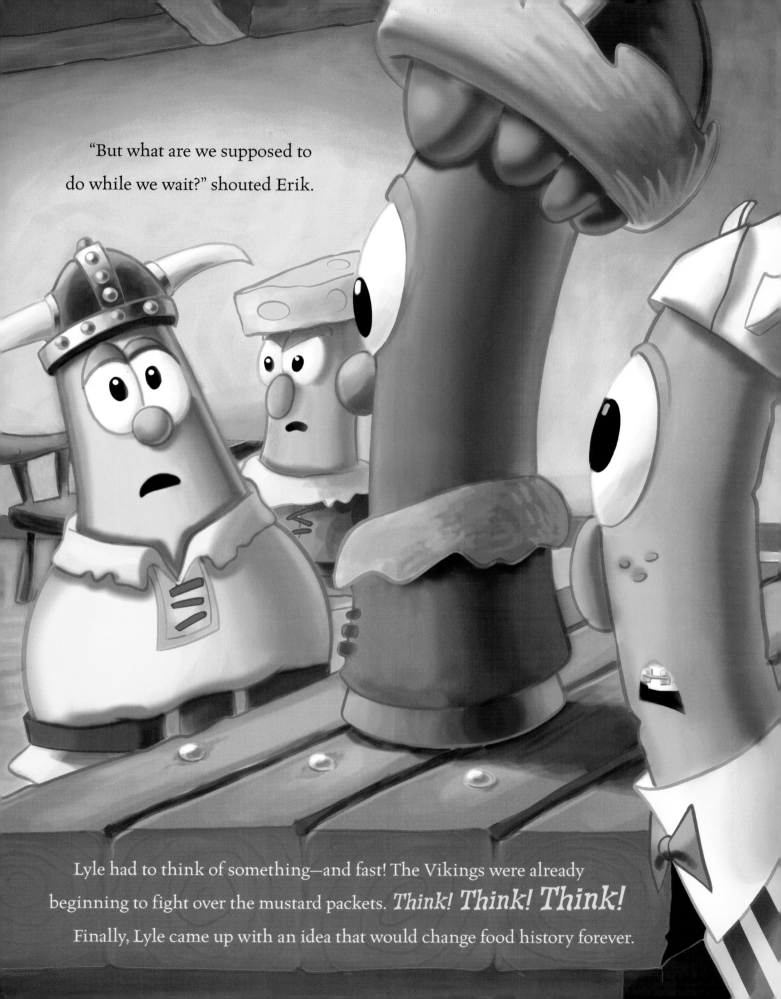

"But what are we supposed to do while we wait?" shouted Erik.

Lyle had to think of something—and fast! The Vikings were already beginning to fight over the mustard packets. *Think! Think! Think!* Finally, Lyle came up with an idea that would change food history forever.

"We'll play a game!" Lyle announced. Hopping down from the counter, he grabbed the only chunk of cheese that did not sink with the ship. "I call the game—*food-ball!*"

Making it up on the spot, Lyle told them that the goal of the game was to take turns. "Each team takes turns running with this cheese food-ball," Lyle said. "The Cheese-Packers get four tries to carry the food-ball across a line. The Vikings will try to tackle the Cheese-Packers to stop them from scoring. Then the Vikings get four tries to score. The Cheese-Packers will try to tackle them."

Warriors *love* tackling.

"What do we get if we win?" asked Bjorn.

Lyle hopped back onto the counter and held a golden soup bowl up high. "The winning team gets this!" he declared. "I call it the Chicken Noodle Souper Bowl!"

"OOOooooooooOOO!" cried both teams.

Lyle marched back and forth like a coach. "Sure, waiting isn't easy," he shouted. "George the Flipper is home sick and the breaks are going against you. But when the waiting gets tough, the tough get waiting! So give it all you've got!

Go out there and play one for the Flipper!"

With a great shout, everyone charged outside onto a frozen field,
where they played the very first food-ball game in history.

The Vikings won the game: 42 to 39. But more important, both teams found out that the game was a lot more fun when the teams took turns with the ball. In fact, the game wouldn't work at all if the two teams didn't wait their turn.

When the food showed up, a surprising thing happened—even though the Vikings and Cheese-Packers were very hungry.

This time, everyone waited in line for the chicken noodle soup *and* they were all very polite.

"After you," Erik said to the big gourd.

"No, you first," said the gourd with a grin.

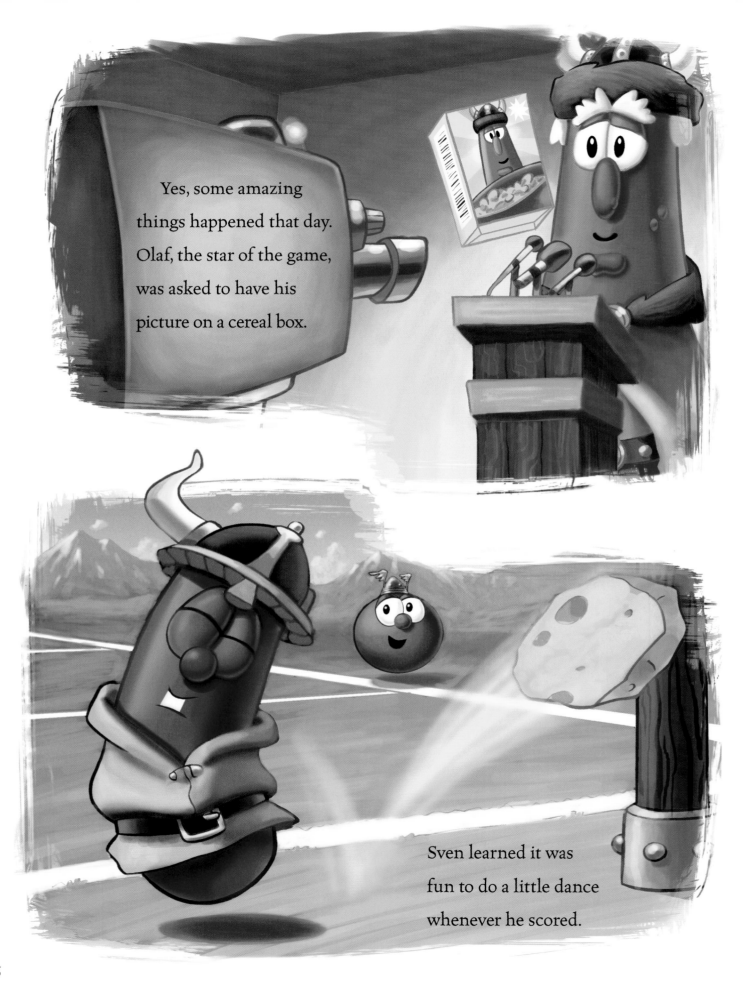

Yes, some amazing things happened that day. Olaf, the star of the game, was asked to have his picture on a cereal box.

Sven learned it was fun to do a little dance whenever he scored.

And Ottar led everyone in a very special fight song:

Cheer, cheer! We're glad that you came!
We've got the cheese ball. Let's play the game!
If the other team is late,
That's quite okay 'cause we've learned to wait!

But the most amazing thing of all was that all the wild warriors
learned that being patient was more fun than bickering.
Now *that's* something to cheer about!

It is better to be patient than to fight . . .
Proverbs 16:32